Ricky Ricotta's Mighty Robot vs. the Stupid Stinkbugs from Saturn

The Sixth Robot Adventure Novel by

DAV PILKEY

Pictures by

MARTIN ONTIVEROS

For Paige Harris Lucas

—D. P.

To ... Ev... ... mentor and f...nd,
wh... ... to walk the wack... ...ath
... of an artist.

—M. O.

Scholastic
An imprint of Scholastic Ltd
Euston House, 24 Eversholt Street
London, NW1 1DB, UK
Registered office: Westfield Road, Southam, Warwickshire, CV47 0RA
SCHOLASTIC and associated logos are trademarks and/or registered trademarks of Scholastic Inc.

First published in the US by Scholastic Inc, 2003
First published in the UK by Scholastic Ltd, 2003
This edition published 2012

Text copyright © Dav Pilkey, 2003
Ilustrations copyright © Martin Ontiveros, 2003

The right of Dav Pilkey and Martin Ontiveros to be identified as the
author and illustrator of this work respectively has been asserted by them.

ISBN 978 1407 10763 9

A CIP catalogue record for this book is available from the British Library.

Printed and bound by CPI Group (UK) Ltd, Croydon, CR0 4YY
Papers used by Scholastic Children's Books are made from wood grown in sustainable forests.

1 3 5 7 9 10 8 6 4 2

www.scholastic.co.uk/zone
www.pilkey.com

Chapters

CHAPTER 1
Ricky and his Robot

One fine day, Ricky Ricotta and his mighty Robot were playing cops and robbers in their yard.

Ricky liked to play the robber because he was good at hiding.

Ricky's mighty Robot liked playing the cop because he was good at finding things.

"Hey, no fair," Ricky laughed.
"You're not allowed to use
X-ray vision!"

10

Soon Ricky's mother came outside.

"Come along, boys," she said. "We are going to your cousin Lucy's house for lunch."

"Aww, man!" said Ricky. "Do we have to go?"

"Yes," said Ricky's mother. "It will be fun."

"But Uncle Freddie always shakes my hand too hard," said Ricky. "And Auntie Ethel always kisses me too much . . . and Cousin Lucy always wants to play princess!"

"Well, we are going anyway," said
Ricky's mother. "So please try to
have some fun."

"We'll go," Ricky sighed, "but we
won't have any fun!"

12

CHAPTER 2

Uncle Freddie and Auntie Ethel

Soon Ricky and his parents arrived at Cousin Lucy's house.

"Hello, Ricky, my boy," said Uncle Freddie. He grabbed Ricky's hand and shook it hard.

"Ow!" said Ricky.

"Come on now," said Uncle Freddie. "Nobody likes a wimpy handshake!"

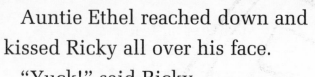

Auntie Ethel reached down and
kissed Ricky all over his face.

"Yuck!" said Ricky.

"Now, now," said Auntie Ethel.
"Everybody loves kisses!"

Ricky's mighty Robot wanted to
say hello, too. He reached down and
shook Uncle Freddie's hand.

"Owza yowza!" shouted Uncle
Freddie.

"Nobody likes a wimpy handshake,"
Ricky giggled.

Then Ricky's Robot gave Auntie Ethel a big, slobbery kiss.

"What's the matter?" Ricky laughed. "I thought you loved kisses!"

Ricky and his mighty Robot flew
into the backyard.

There was Lucy, having a tea party
with her pets.

"Wow!" cried Ricky. "Look how big your Jurassic Jackrabbits got!"

"They like to eat," said Lucy. "So I named them Fudgie, Cupcake, and Waffles."

Ricky rolled his eyes.

"Let's play princess!" Lucy said.

"No way!" said Ricky.

"Oh, come on," Lucy begged. "I'll be the beautiful princess, and you can be the ugly prince. Fudgie, Cupcake, and Waffles will be our royal ponies, and your Robot can be the big, brave knight."

"What part of no way don't you understand?" asked Ricky.

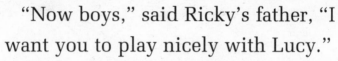

"Now boys," said Ricky's father, "I want you to play nicely with Lucy."

"Rats!" said Ricky. "This is turning out to be a very bad day."

But what Ricky didn't know was that things were about to get much, much worse.

CHAPTER 3

Sergeant Stinkbug

More than 750 million kilometres away, there was a polluted planet called Saturn, which was overrun with stupid, smelly stinkbugs.

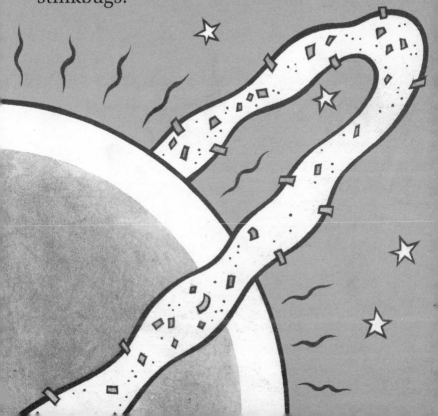

Everywhere you looked, trash filled
the streets. . .

. . .garbage gunked up the rivers. . .

. . .and the factories puffed out so much pollution, it formed a toxic ring of smoke around the whole planet.

But of all the stupid, smelly creatures on Saturn, there was no one stupider or smellier than evil Sergeant Stinkbug. He was the ruler of Saturn, and he was the worst litterbug of all.

Every day when Sergeant Stinkbug was done eating, he threw his dirty dishes out of the window.

Every night when he was through watching his favourite shows, he tossed his TV out of the window.

And every morning when he was
finished sleeping in his bed . . .
well, you get the idea.

Usually, Sergeant Stinkbug loved
his smelly, toxic planet. But today
as he strolled through Pollution
Parkway, he got fed up.

"This place is a DUMP!" he
shouted.

"I want to find a new planet that
I can junk up!"

So Sergeant Stinkbug gathered
his stinky subjects, climbed aboard
his Giant Spaceship, and headed
for Earth.

CHAPTER 4

The Princess of Earth

When the Giant Spaceship reached Earth, Sergeant Stinkbug spoke to his armies.

"Listen up, you stinkers," said the evil Sergeant. "First we must find the king of Earth and kidnap him. Then we will take over the planet!"

The Stupid Stinkbugs searched
through their Super-Sonic Spy
Scope, but they could not find a
king. They looked all over Earth,
but they couldn't even find a queen.

"Duh, look!" said one of the
Stupid Stinkbugs finally. "I think I
see a princess!"

The Super-Sonic Spy Scope zoomed in on Lucy, who was standing on the picnic table giving orders.

"You guys have to protect me," Lucy said, "so the bad guys don't steal all of my precious rubies!"

"A-HA!" cried Sergeant Stinkbug.
"I'll kidnap that princess and steal all
of those rubies she was talking about.
Then we'll all take over the planet!"

So Sergeant Stinkbug got into his
Attack Pod and headed for Lucy's
house.

CHAPTER 5

The Picnic

Soon it was time for lunch. Ricky's aunt and uncle brought food out to everybody. Then they went back inside to eat with Ricky's parents.

Fudgie, Cupcake, Waffles, Ricky, and his mighty Robot all dove into their grilled cheese sandwiches.

"C'mon you guys," Lucy whined. "Let's play before we eat."

Suddenly, Sergeant Stinkbug
showed up. He lowered the
Automatic Snatcher Arm on his
Attack Pod and grabbed Lucy.

"Hey, look everybody," cried Lucy. "A bad guy is trying to steal my rubies!"

"Yeah, right," said Ricky, who didn't even bother to turn around.

"C'mon you guys!" cried Lucy. "Stop eating and save me from this evil space-bug!"

"Boy," said Ricky, "that kid sure has a vivid imagination."

CHAPTER 6

Lucy in the Sky with Rubies

Sergeant Stinkbug carried Lucy high into the air and demanded to know where all the rubies were.

"They're right here on my crown, you big dummy!" said Lucy.

"Those aren't real," said Sergeant Stinkbug. "You just drew those on with crayons!"

"You better put me down before my Jurassic Jackrabbits beat you up!" said Lucy.

40

"Ooh! I'm so scared!" mocked
Sergeant Stinkbug. "Did you draw
them with crayons, too?"

"No," said Lucy. "They're real. . .

. . .and they're right behind you!"

Sergeant Stinkbug turned and saw
Fudgie, Cupcake, and Waffles.

"Help!" he screamed. The
Automatic Snatcher Arm let go of
Lucy and she fell . . .

. . .right into the mighty Robot's hand.

"Nice catch!" said Lucy.

Ricky's mighty Robot grabbed Sergeant Stinkbug's Attack Pod and held it tightly.

"All right," said Ricky, "what's going on here?"

"Ooh, nothing," said Sergeant Stinkbug, as he reached down and pushed the EMERGENCY ATTACK button on his wristwatch.

Suddenly, the Giant Spaceship floating above Earth opened up. Two Warrior Stinkbugs flew out of the spaceship and down to Sergeant Stinkbug's side. They were ready to attack.

CHAPTER 7

The Big Fight

Sergeant Stinkbug reached into a bag and grabbed two round gumballs.

"My Grow-Big Gumballs should do the trick," laughed the evil Sergeant. "Here you go, my uglies!"

He threw the gumballs into the Warrior Stinkbugs' mouths.

The Warriors chewed and chewed, and they grew bigger and bigger and bigger. Then they attacked Ricky's Robot.

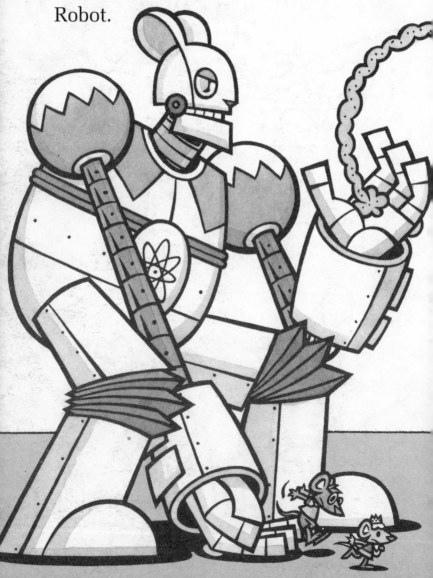

49

The Stupid Stinkbugs started their assault with a super-smashin' swinger stomp.

But Ricky's Robot bounced back with a bone-bustin' blast from his bionic belt buckle.

Then he finished his fight
for freedom with a free-flyin'
foot in their funky faces.

CHAPTER 8

Captured

Ricky's mighty Robot was victorious, but not for long. Sergeant Stinkbug leaned out of his Attack Pod and tossed more Grow-Big Gumballs into the mouths of his Warrior Stinkbugs.

As the Warriors chewed, they grew
and grew and grew some more.

Soon the Warriors were ten times
bigger than Ricky's mighty Robot.
They grabbed Ricky's Robot in
their gigantic fists and prepared to
pound him to pieces.

"We've got to save my Robot!"
cried Ricky.

Together, Ricky, Lucy, and Waffles
worked out a plan.

Fudgie and Cupcake wanted to
help, too, but they couldn't fly.

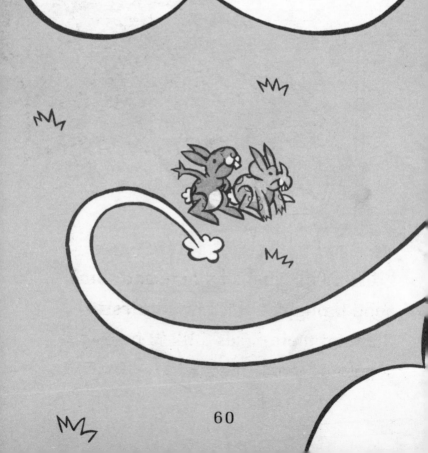

"You boys just stay here and think good thoughts!" said Lucy, kissing them on their noses. "We'll be back soon, and everything will be fine!"

Ricky, Lucy, and Waffles flew up to Sergeant Stinkbug's Attack Pod.

"Let go of my Robot right now," yelled Ricky, "or you'll be sorry!"

"You're the one who's going to be sorry," laughed Sergeant Stinkbug. He pressed a button on his ship and sprayed our three heroes with Super-Stenchy Stink-Gas.

The Automatic Snatcher Arm
reached out, grabbed Ricky, Lucy,
and Waffles, and held them tightly.
Then Sergeant Stinkbug called for
his troops.

The Giant Spaceship opened up.
Suddenly, hundreds of Attack Pods
poured out, lining up in formation.

CHAPTER 9

Fudgie and Cupcake to the Rescue

Fudgie and Cupcake watched the horror unfold above their heads. It looked like the end of the world. They knew they couldn't fly, but they still had to do something.

So Fudgie and Cupcake ran up the leg of one of the Warrior Stinkbugs. They dashed across his thigh, then bolted up his back.

Finally, the two Jurassic Jackrabbits scurried up to the Warrior Stinkbug's shoulder and jumped.

Down they fell until they crash-landed on Sergeant Stinkbug's Attack Pod.

The collision caused Sergeant
Stinkbug to flip out of his Pod, but
Cupcake caught him.

"Hooray for Fudgie and Cupcake!"
shouted Ricky and Lucy.

Fudgie rummaged through the Attack Pod until he found the Grow-Big Gumballs.

"Good boy, Fudgie!" said Ricky. "Now toss 'em here!"

Fudgie wagged his fluffy tail and dropped the bag of gumballs into Ricky's hands. Ricky popped six gumballs into his mouth, then chewed and chewed. . .

. . .and grew and grew and grew!

Now Ricky was as big as the Warrior
Stinkbugs. He grabbed his mighty
Robot out of their hands and tucked
him into his shirt pocket.

"Don't worry, Mighty Robot," said
Ricky, "it's my turn to save the day!"

CHAPTER 10

The Big Battle
(IN FLIP-O-RAMA™)

ꓚ·RaMa
HERE'S HOW IT WORKS!

STEP 1
Place your *left* hand inside the dotted lines marked "LEFT HAND HERE." Hold the book open *flat*.

STEP 2
Grasp the right-hand page with your *right* thumb and index finger (inside the dotted lines marked "Right Thumb Here").

STEP 3
Now *quickly* flip the right-hand page back and forth until the picture appears to be *animated*.

(For extra fun, try adding your own sound effects!)

FLIP-O-RAMA 1

(pages 79 and 81)

Remember, flip only page 79.
While you are flipping, make sure
you can see the picture on page 79
and the one on page 81.
If you flip quickly, the two
pictures will start to look like
<u>one</u> animated picture.

Don't forget to add
your own sound effects!

LEFT HAND HERE

The Stupid Stinkbugs
Attacked.

FLIP-O-RAMA 2

(pages 83 and 85)

Remember, flip only page 83.
While you are flipping, make sure
you can see the picture on page 83
and the one on page 85.
If you flip quickly, the two
pictures will start to look like
<u>one</u> animated picture.

Don't forget to add
your own sound effects!

LEFT HAND HERE

Ricky Fought Back.

RIGHT
THUMB
HERE

Ricky Fought Back.

FLIP-O-RAMA 3

(pages 87 and 89)

Remember, flip only page 87.
While you are flipping, make sure
you can see the picture on page 87
and the one on page 89.
If you flip quickly, the two
pictures will start to look like
<u>one</u> animated picture.

Don't forget to add
your own sound effects!

LEFT HAND HERE

The Stupid Stinkbugs
Battled Hard.

RIGHT
THUMB
HERE

The Stupid Stinkbugs
Battled Hard.

FLIP-O-RAMA 4

(pages 91 and 93)

Remember, flip only page 91.
While you are flipping, make sure
you can see the picture on page 91
and the one on page 93.
If you flip quickly, the two
pictures will start to look like
<u>one</u> animated picture.

Don't forget to add
your own sound effects!

LEFT HAND HERE

Ricky Battled Harder.

RIGHT
THUMB
HERE

Ricky Battled Harder.

FLIP-O-RAMA 5

(pages 95 and 97)

Remember, flip only page 95.
While you are flipping, make sure
you can see the picture on page 95
and the one on page 97.
If you flip quickly, the two
pictures will start to look like
<u>one</u> animated picture.

Don't forget to add
your own sound effects!

LEFT HAND HERE

Ricky Ricotta
Won the War.

95

Ricky Ricotta
Won the War.

CHAPTER 11

The Final Attack

Ricky had won his battle with the giant Warrior Stinkbugs.

But Sergeant Stinkbug still had one more trick up his sleeve.

He pressed a button on his wristwatch and called for his Attack Pod Troops to attack.

Suddenly, hundreds of Attack Pods started zooming towards Earth.

"Oh, NO!" cried Ricky. "There are too many of them! How will I ever stop them all?"

Just then, a giant finger emerged from a cloud and tapped Ricky on his shoulder. It was Lucy. She had chewed up the rest of the bag of gumballs when nobody was looking.

"I couldn't help it," said Lucy. "I love gumballs!"

Lucy reached into outer space
and opened up the Giant Spaceship.
With it, she scooped up all of the
tiny Attack Pods. Then she shoved
the two Warrior Stinkbugs inside.

105

CHAPTER 12

Just Desserts

Fudgie and Waffles found a bag of Super-Shrinking Saltwater Taffy inside Sergeant Stinkbug's Attack Pod.

They gave the bag to Ricky's Robot, and he fed it to Ricky and Lucy.

Soon, the two cousins had shrunk
back to their normal sizes.

Together, the six friends
flew Sergeant Stinkbug to the
Squeakyville Jail.

Then they zoomed back to Lucy's house just in time for dessert.

The grown-ups brought out big slices of chocolate-chip cheesecake for everybody.

"We heard loud noises out here,"
said Auntie Ethel.

"What have you kids been up to?"
asked Uncle Freddie.

"Well, a bad guy tried to steal my rubies," said Lucy, "but Ricky's Robot beat up the Stinkbugs. Then Fudgie found some gum and I grew big and clobbered the Attack Pods and. . . "

"Boy," said Ricky's mother, "those kids sure have vivid imaginations!"

"I know that Lucy gets on your nerves sometimes," Ricky's dad whispered, "but thank you for being nice to her anyway."

"No problem," said Ricky. . .

. . . "that's what friends are for!"

HOW TO DRAW RICKY

1.

2.

3.

4.

5.

6.

7.

8.

9.

10.

11.

12.

HOW TO DRAW RICKY'S ROBOT

1.

2.

3.

4.

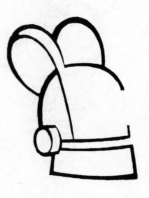

5.

6.

7.

8.

9.

10.

11.

12.

HOW TO DRAW SERGEANT STINKBUG

1.

2.

3.

4.

5.

6.

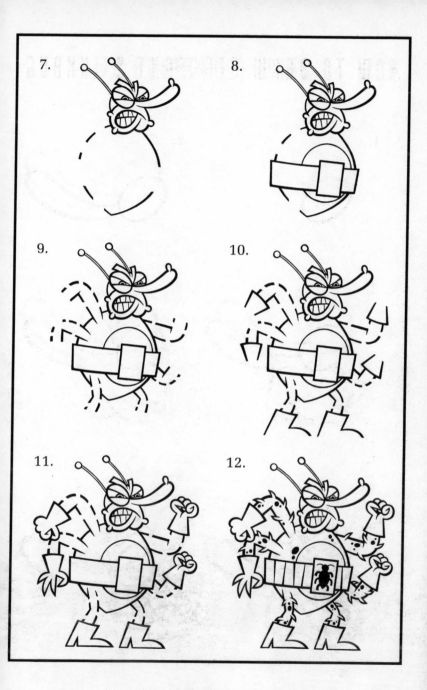

HOW TO DRAW A WARRIOR STINKBUG

1.

2.

3.

4.

5.

6.

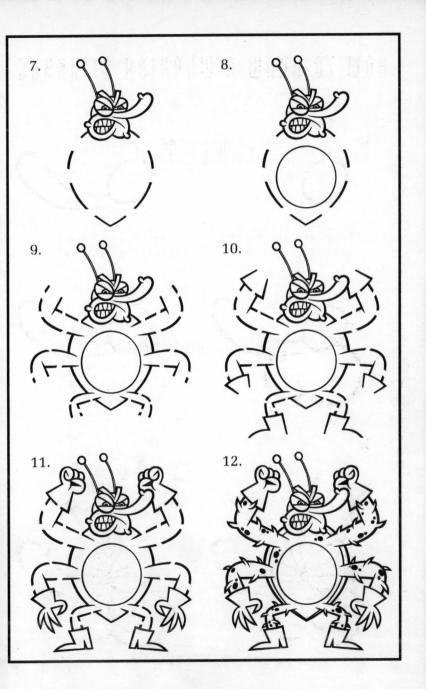

COMING SOON:

Ricky Ricotta's Mighty Robot

vs.

The Uranium Unicorns from Uranus

About the Author and Illustrator

DAV PILKEY created his first stories as comic books while he was in elementary school. In 1997, he wrote and illustrated his first adventure novel for children, *The Adventures of Captain Underpants*, which received rave reviews and was an instant bestseller – as were all the books that followed in the series. Dav is also the creator of numerous award-winning picture books. He and his dog live in Eugene, Oregon.

It was a stroke of luck when Dav discovered the work of artist **MARTIN ONTIVEROS**. Dav knew that Martin was just the right illustrator for the *Ricky Ricotta's Mighty Robot* series. Martin has loved drawing since he was a kid. He lives in Portland, Oregon. He has a lot of toys, which he shares with his young son, Felix.

Visit Dav Pilkey's Extra-Crunchy
Web Site O'Fun at:
www.pilkey.com